W9-DEE-616

Science Experiments with Simple Machines

Simple Experiments with

Pulleys

Chris Oxlade

WINDMILL
BOOKS
New York

Published in 2014 by Windmill Books, An Imprint of Rosen Publishing
29 East 21st Street, New York, NY 10010

Produced for Windmill by Calcium Creative Ltd
Editors for Calcium Creative Ltd: Sarah Eason and Jennifer Sanderson
Designer: Emma DeBanks

Photo Credits: Cover: Istockphoto: Jordi Ramisa. Inside: Emma DeBanks 25,
26, 27; Dreamstime: Ankevanwyk 6, Fotokate 21, Gail Johnson 5, Marcopolo
12–13, Vibeimages 8; Shutterstock: Alephcomo 15, Aragami12345s 14, Steve
Estvanik 20, Fotofermer 4, Holbox 9, Ruslan Kokarev 24, Murat5234 17, Andrei
Orlov 16, PavelSh 23, TFoxFoto 22, Ventdusud 7, Edwin Verin 1, 29; Tudor
Photography: 10, 11, 18, 19.

Library of Congress Cataloging-in-Publication Data

Oxlade, Chris.
Simple experiments with pulleys / by Chris Oxlade.
pages cm — (Science experiments with simple machines)
Includes index.
ISBN 978-1-61533-751-4 (library binding) — ISBN 978-1-61533-819-1 (pbk.) —
ISBN 978-1-61533-820-7 (6-pack)
1. Pulleys—Experiments—Juvenile literature. 2. Force and energy—
Experiments—Juvenile literature. I. Title.
TJ1103.O954 2014
621.8—dc23
2013003809

Manufactured in the United States of America

CPSIA Compliance Information: Batch #BS13WM: For Further Information contact Windmill Books, New York, New York at 1-866-478-0556

Contents

Simple Machines

What do you think of when you hear the word "machine?" Perhaps you imagine a car, a robot, or even a lawn mower. Machines are things that make our lives easier, by helping us do jobs. Cars, robots, and lawn mowers are complicated machines made up of thousands of parts. However, many machines are very simple. They have only one or two parts. **Pulleys** are one type of simple machine.

Types of Simple Machines

There are six types of simple machines. Pulleys are one. The others are **wheel and axles**, **levers**, **screws**, **wedges**, and **inclined planes**. Some of these machines do not really look like machines. Some do not have any moving parts. However, they still help us do jobs in our everyday lives.

This is a simple pulley wheel. It is the type of pulley that rock climbers use to lift their equipment.

On a rescue helicopter, a pulley helps to lift casualties from the sea.

What Is a Pulley?

A pulley is a wheel with a rope that passes around it. When the rope is pulled, the wheel moves around. Wheels with belts around them and cogs with chains around them are also considered pulleys. Whenever you ride your bicycle, pulleys are helping you. In this book, you will find many examples of pulleys in action. There are also some interesting experiments for you to do. Try them out and discover for yourself how pulleys work.

Pulley Parts

A simple pulley is made up of two main parts. They include a pulley wheel that can spin around, and a rope that goes around it. One cannot work without the other. A pulley wheel has a groove around its rim. This stops the rope from sliding from side to side. The groove also helps to grip the rope.

Pulley Blocks

A pulley wheel has an axle through its center so that it can spin around freely. The axle is supported by a casing. Together the wheel, axle, and case are called a pulley **block**. Pulley blocks can have two or more pulley wheels. The job of a pulley wheel is to let the rope move easily through the pulley block.

This pulley block contains two pulley wheels.

A cable car uses a pulley system to lift people up a mountain.

Pulleys Without Wheels

You can make a pulley without a wheel. For example, you could put the rope through a smooth metal hoop. However, there would be **friction** between the rope and the metal, and the rope would not move easily.

Pushes and Pulls

In this book you will see the words "**force**," "effort," and "**load**." A force is a push or a pull. Simple machines change the direction or **magnitude** of forces. An effort is a force that you make on a simple machine. The load is the **weight** or other force that a machine moves.

Simple Pulleys

The simplest way of using a pulley is to fix a pulley block in one place and put a rope around it. Then, a pull on one end of the rope makes a pull on the other end of the rope. The pulley changes the direction of the pull. It does not make the pull any larger.

A flagpole has a pulley at the top for raising the flag.

Lifting a Load

One of the simplest uses of a pulley is to lift a heavy object, such as a bucket of cement, up to where it is needed. This might be lifting building materials up a scaffold. To do this, a pulley block is attached to the top of the scaffolding, and a rope is put over the pulley wheel. The bucket is attached to one end of the rope, so that a construction worker can pull on the other end.

Here is a pulley that is used to lift buckets of water from a well.

Using Force

In the example of a worker pulling a bucket up a scaffold, the effort is the pull the worker makes on the rope and the load is the weight of the bucket. The worker has to pull down with the same force as the bucket pulls down on the other end of the rope. The pulley makes lifting the bucket easier because the worker can pull downward on the rope, using his or her weight to help.

Lifting with a Pulley

This experiment will show you how a simple pulley can make it easier to lift objects. The pulley changes the direction of a pull, from pulling down to pulling up.

You Will Need:

- Two old CDs (or DVDs)
- Corrugated cardboard
- Pencil
- A pair of scissors
- Glue
- String
- A weight (such as a bag of marbles or crayons)

1 Put a CD on some corrugated cardboard and draw around it with a pencil. Draw another circle around ¾ inch (19 mm) inside the first. Cut out this circle to make a disk. Cut a hole around ½ inch (13 mm) wide in the center of the disk.

10

2 Glue your disk to the CD, making sure it is in the center. Now glue another CD to the cardboard, and allow the glue to dry. This is your pulley wheel.

3 Tie your weight to the end of a piece of string and place it on the floor. Put the pulley wheel onto your finger, then put the string into the groove of the pulley wheel. Pull down on the string to lift the weight!

So Simple!

This is the simplest use of a pulley wheel. The pulley changed the direction of the pull you made on the string. Pulling down on the string lifted up the weight up.

making Forces Bigger

A single pulley block and a rope do not change the size of a force. We can add more pulley wheels to make more complicated pulley systems that do make forces bigger. These systems are called compound pulleys. With a compound pulley, you can overcome a huge load with a small effort.

Two-Block Pulley

Let's start by looking at a compound pulley with two pulley blocks. Remember the single pulley system for lifting a bucket of cement from page 8? Imagine the same thing with two pulley blocks. The second block is attached to the bucket. One end of the rope is attached to the top block. Then the rope goes around the lower pulley, back up over the top pulley, and down again. When the worker pulls on this end of the rope, the bottom pulley moves up, lifting the weight.

Here is a simple compound pulley put to use on a crane.

Half the Effort

With a two-block pulley system, you have to pull 2 feet (60 cm) of rope through your hands to lift the bucket 1 foot (30 cm). The advantage is that the pulley system doubles the effort you make. If the bucket weighs 20 pounds (9 kg), you will only need to pull down with an effort of 10 pounds (4.5 kg) to lift it.

Compound Pulleys

Compound pulleys help us lift or move heavy objects with only a small effort. In most systems there are two pulley blocks. Each block has one or more pulleys wheels. The rope is attached to one block, and goes back and forth between the blocks until it is wrapped around all of the wheels. This creates a **block and tackle.**

Adding Pulleys

We've seen that a compound pulley with one pulley wheel at each end doubles the effort you make. However, you do have to pull 2 feet (60 cm) of rope through your hands to lift a load by just 1 foot (30 cm). What happens if you add another pulley to make a three-pulley system? For this, you need an extra pulley wheel in one of the blocks. Now, the pulley system triples the effort you make on the rope, making it even easier to lift the load. However, you do have to pull 3 feet (90 cm) of rope through your hands to lift a load by just 1 foot (30 cm).

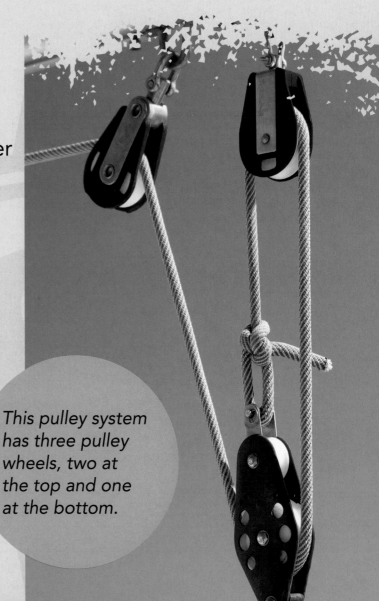

This pulley system has three pulley wheels, two at the top and one at the bottom.

14

More and More

You can keep adding pulley wheels to make it easier and easier to lift a load. However, each time you have to pull more rope through. Block and tackles for lifting very big loads, such as the ones on construction cranes, might have as many as 10 pulley wheels on each block.

This crane uses several pulley wheels to lift heavy loads.

Pulleys Afloat

You can see many pulleys at work on boats. Pulleys help sailors put up their sails and control the position of those sails. They also pull, lift, and tighten parts of a boat to make the boat go faster. Pulleys are found on both the smallest sailboats and the biggest luxury yachts.

Raising the Sails

There are pulley wheels and blocks at the top of a sailboat's mast. Ropes or wires go from the base of the mast, over the pulleys, and back down again. Some pulleys are used to pull the tops of the sails up the mast. The sail is tied to one end and the sailor pulls down on the other end to raise the sail.

A pulley holds the boat's sails in position.

This boat is lifted and lowered into the water using two sets of pulleys.

Controlling the Sails

Sails propel a sailboat along as the wind blows on them. The wind presses on the sails, and the sailor has to pull on them to stop them from swinging sideways and spilling the wind. In a strong wind, the sailor has to pull hard. He or she does this with a pulley system. A pull on the rope makes a bigger pull on the sails.

A Pulley System

This experiment will show you the power of pulleys. You can make a simple pulley system from broom handles and rope. Try using it to give yourself super-strength to overpower your friends and family!

1 Put two broom handles on the floor, parallel to each other and around 18 inches (45 cm) apart. Tie one end of your rope firmly to one of the handles. Feed the rope around the second handle and back over the first handle.

2 Ask two people to lift up one handle each. Ask them to try to pull the handles apart. At the same time, pull on the free end of the rope. Can you pull the handles together?

3 Now, wrap the rope around the first handle and around second handle again. Then, try pulling your friends together again. Is it easier this time?

So Simple!

The broom handles and rope made a simple pulley system. In step 2, the system made your pull on the rope twice as big. In step 3, it made your pull four times as big, making it easier to pull your friends toward each other.

Pulleys in the Past

Nobody knows exactly when people started to use pulleys. We think that the simple pulley was probably invented around 3,500 years ago, in an area called Mesopotamia, where Iraq is today.

Inventing the Pulley

The famous mathematician Archimedes, who lived in ancient Greece more than 2,200 years ago, invented the compound pulley. It is said that Archimedes demonstrated his pulley by moving a floating warship packed with soldiers by himself. The ancient Greeks, and the ancient Romans, also put pulleys to work in cranes. Pulleys and other simple machines helped them lift and move heavy objects by human power.

More than 800 years ago, Notre Dame Cathedral, in Paris, France, was built using cranes with pulleys.

All the pulleys on this ship control its sails.

The Age of Pulleys

Steamships were developed in the nineteenth century. For hundreds of years before that, most ships were powered by sails. Some of these ships were enormous, with dozens of heavy sails. Pulleys were the only way that the crews of these ships could hoist and control the sails.

Man-powered pulleys were used in factories and in mills to lift heavy materials to the upper floors. As in Roman times, pulleys were used on building sites to lift stone and other building materials. Craftsmen built stone cathedrals using simple machines like these.

Pulley Belts

Pulley wheels are not just used to lift and move heavy objects in pulley systems. They are also used to transfer movement from one place to another. This means we can use pulleys to make one wheel turn by turning another wheel. We do this by putting a belt around the two pulley wheels. Then, as one of the wheels turns, the belt makes the other wheel turn, too.

Strong and Flexible

Pulley belts are normally made of rubber. Rubber is strong and **flexible**, so it does not stretch or snap, but it does bend as it goes around the pulley wheels. The rubber also creates friction when it is touching the pulley wheels, so the belt does not slip when the wheels are turning. Belts are often triangular, and fit neatly into a triangular groove in the rims of the pulley wheels.

These two pulley wheels are linked by a pulley belt.

The chain passes around cogs on the rear wheel of a bicycle.

Cogs and Chains

Bicycles have a pulley belt to make the rear wheel turn. Instead of a rubber belt and grooved wheels, they have a metal chain and cogs, or wheels with teeth around the rim. The chain is made of small sections joined together, and holes in the chain fit over teeth on the cogs. The chain is very strong and the cogs stop it from slipping as they turn.

Changing Forces

We have seen that pulley blocks and ropes can make an effort much larger. Two pulley wheels and a belt can change forces, too. To make this happen, we make one of the pulley wheels larger than the other. When the smaller wheel is turned, the belt turns the second wheel, but more slowly than the first. The effort used to turn the first wheel makes a larger force on the second wheel.

Increasing Force

A washing machine offers a simple example of a pulley and belt making a force larger. The machine's heavy washing drum is turned by an electric motor. There is a rubber belt that goes around a small pulley wheel on the motor's shaft and around a large pulley wheel on the back of the drum. It takes many turns of the motor to turn the drum once. This means that a small push from the motor can make a large force to start the drum turning.

Inside a washing machine, the motor at the bottom of the machine drives the drum at the top.

Can you see the pulley wheels on this bicycle's gear system?

Chains and Gears

A bicycle has cogs and a chain that make the rear wheel turn when you pedal. On a bicycle with **gears**, the rear wheel has several cogs on it, each a different size. When you change gear, the chain moves from one cog to another. Choosing a larger cog makes the wheel turn fewer times, but makes it easier to pedal.

Bicycle Pulleys

This is an experiment to test how changing gears on bicycle makes it easier or more difficult to turn the bicycle's wheel. The front cog, rear cog, and chain make a pulley system.

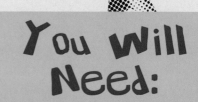
1 First, you need to lift the back wheel of your bicycle off the ground, so that you can turn the wheel without the bicycle moving along. You can do this by putting the bicycle upside down, resting on its seat and handlebars. Use old towels or cushions to protect them.

2 Select the gear with the lowest number (you will have to keep the pedals turning to change gear). Turn the pedals with your hand to make the rear wheel turn. How hard do you have to push to make the wheel turn?

3 Now, change to the gear with the highest number. How hard do you have to push this time to move the rear wheel?

So Simple!

You should have found that it was easier to make the rear wheel turn at the lowest gear. This was when the chain was on the biggest rear cog. The push needed to move the wheel depended on the size of the rear cog.

Amazing Machines

Pulleys are incredibly useful. They make our lives easier by increasing the effort we make. They let us lift and move objects that are too heavy to move by hand. They help us harness strong forces, such as the wind in sailboat sails. Other pulleys work with pulley belts and chains. They turn things, such as washing machine drums and bicycle wheels.

What Did You Learn?

What did you learn about pulleys from the experiments in this book? Can you think up any pulley experiments of your own?

In Big Machines

Pulleys are simple machines that can be useful on their own. However, we also find them in complicated machines. Many machines with moving parts have pulleys working away inside. These complex machines include construction cranes, hoists in factories, cable cars, motorcycles, printers (where pulley belts move the printer head), vacuum cleaners, and gym machines.

Can't Live Without Them

Humans have been using pulleys for thousands of years. They might be simple, but they are so useful that it would be much harder to live without them. You can find pulleys in your home, in vehicles, and on construction sites. Keep an eye out for pulleys wherever you go!

Most large cranes, found on construction sites, rely on pulleys to work.

Glossary

block (BLOK) A pulley wheel mounted on an axle inside a case.

block and tackle (BLOK AND TA-kul) A pulley system with a block at each end, each containing one or more pulley wheels.

flexible (FLEK-sih-bul) Able to bend.

force (FORS) A push or pull.

friction (FRIK-shin) The force that tries to stop two surfaces from sliding over each other.

gears (GEERZ) Wheels with teeth around the rim, so that they can interlock with other gears.

inclined planes (in-KLYND-PLAYNS) Slopes used as simple machines.

levers (LEH-vurs) Rods or bars that move around points called fulcrums.

load (LOHD) The push or pull that a pulley overcomes, which may be the weight of an object.

magnitude (MAG-nih-tood) The measurement of something's strength.

pulleys (PU-leez) Wheels with ropes around them that work as simple machines.

screws (SKROOZ) Simple machines with inclined planes wrapped around cyclinders.

wedges (WEJ-ez) Triangular objects used as simple machines.

weight (WAYT) The force of gravity on an object, which pulls the object downward.

wheel and axles (WEEL AND AK-sulz) Simple machines made up of disks with fixed bars running through their centers.

Read More

To learn more about pulleys, check out these interesting books:

Dahl, Michael. *Pull, Lift, and Lower: A Book About Pulleys.* Amazing Science: Simple Machines. Mankato, MN: Picture Window Books, 2002.

De Medeiros, James. *Pulleys.* Science Matters. New York: Weigl Publishers, 2009.

Gosman, Gillian. *Pulleys in Action.* Simple Machines at Work. New York: PowerKids Press, 2011.

Walker, Sally M., and Roseann Feldmann. *Put Pulleys to the Test.* Searchlight Books: How Do Simple Machines Work? Minneapolis, MN: Lerner Publications, 2012.

Yasuda, Anita. *Explore Simple Machines!* Explore Your World. White River Junction, Vermont: Nomad Press, 2011.

Websites

For web resources related to the subject of this book, go to: www.windmillbooks.com/weblinks and select this book's title.

Index